A TIME TO CLIMB

by
Wendy Wax

illustrated by
Artful Doodlers Ltd.

SCHOLASTIC INC.
New York Toronto London Auckland Sydney
Mexico City New Delhi Hong Kong Buenos Aires

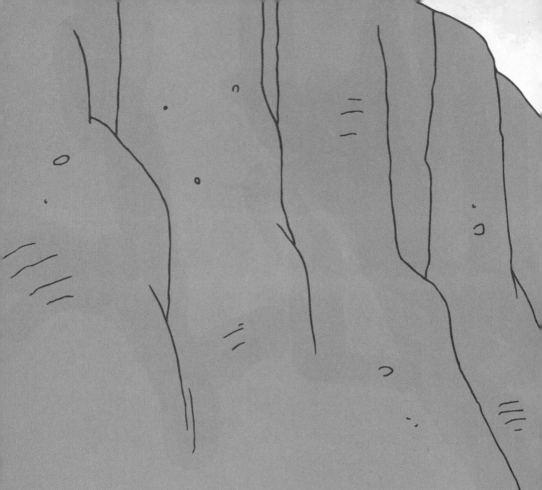

KLASKY
CSUPO INC.
Based on the TV series *Nickelodeon Rocket Power*® created by Klasky Csupo, Inc. as seen on Nickelodeon®

ISBN 0-439-62348-0

12 11 10 9 8 7 6 5 4 3 2 1   4 5 6 7 8 9/0

Printed in the U.S.A.

First Scholastic printing, January 2004

Twister looked up at Super Slab,

the steepest climbing rock in Ocean Shores.

"This is perfect!" he said, as he raced over

to Otto's house.

"I want you both in my rock climbing video," Twister told Otto and Reggie. "We can film at Super Slab next Saturday." "Cool!" said Otto.

"Dad, have you climbed it?" Reggie asked Ray.

"I sure have," said Ray, "and I will give you all a crash course in climbing."

"What about Sam?" Reggie asked Twister.
"I am making a **video**, not a **Squid-eo**,"
Twister said. "But I guess you can be
an extra, Sammy."

The next morning everyone met
at an indoor climbing wall.
"You need to practice, practice, practice,"
Ray said. "That goes for you too, Twister."
"I will be okay," said Twister.

By lunchtime Otto and Reggie had mastered most of the climbing wall. Sam was still on his first trip up, climbing very slowly.

"Hey, Squidman!" Twister called loudly.

"Aaaahhhh!" Sam cried, as he fell

to the mat.

Later Sam went to the Shore Shack.

"I will never be a good climber,"

he told Tito.

"Rock climbing is all about you and the rock," Tito said. "You breathe, the rock does not. How would you like me to coach you?"

"That would be great!" said Sam.

The next day Ray went over hand signals. "They are good to know in case we are too far away to hear each other," he said. "What's the signal for **tighten up on the rope**?" Ray asked Twister. "Uh . . . what?" Twister asked.

Sam practiced hard all week.

But no one knew that.

Tito taught Sam to take his time to climb, to breathe deeply, and to focus.

The more Sam practiced, the stronger he got
and the better he was at climbing.

On Saturday, Ray drove Reggie, Otto, and Twister to Super Slab.

"Has anyone seen Sam?" Otto asked.

"I have not seen him all week," said Twister.

"I feel bad," said Reggie. "I meant to call him."

But when they got to Super Slab,

Sam was waiting for them.

"Sam!" Reggie cried. "We missed you!"

"Thanks for coming to watch," said Otto.

"I would not miss it," Sam said, grinning.

Ray began to climb up Super Slab.

He had tools to plant in the rocks.

The kids could use them for support

when they climbed up.

"This is tough!" Ray yelled. "I'm sweating

buckets."

"I wish Ray would cruise right up,"
Twister said. "I have to save some film
for Otto and Reggie."

"Let him go at his own pace," Sam said.
Twister rolled his eyes.

When Ray reached the first pitch,
Reggie attached his trailing rope
to her harness and began to climb.

"Come on, Reggie," Twister called.

"Let's see some fancy footwork."

"Leave her alone," Sam said.

"She has to focus."

"And I have to shoot an exciting video,"

Twister said, sighing.

It was Otto's turn. He climbed up smoothly, but then he slowed down to catch his breath.

"No way!" Twister groaned.

"Reggie was faster."

"Rock climbing is not about who is better,"
Sam said. "It's about you and the rock.
You breathe. The rock does not."

"That's weird, Squid," Twister said.

At last it was Twister's turn to climb.

Sam helped him tie Otto's rope to his harness.

But Twister had not listened to Ray all week.

And up on the rock he missed a foothold—

and fell!

Ray tugged on the rope, breaking Twister's fall.
"Let me down!" Twister cried. He tried to
remember the hand signal for **down**,
but signaled **up** instead.
Up, up, up he went, feeling dizzy.

Luckily Sam knew the signal for **down** and sent it to Ray. Down, down, down Twister went until he landed safely on the ground.

"At least you tried," Sam said to Twister.
Sam untied Otto's rope from Twister's
harness and tied it to his own.
"What are you doing?" asked Twister.
"I'm getting ready to climb," Sam said,
signaling to Ray.

27

"That's it, Sammy!" Otto shouted as Sam climbed up toward them. "Looking good!" Reggie yelled. "Incredible!" shouted Ray.

Twister quickly grabbed his camera.

"Way to go, Squidman!" he shouted.

Later at the Shore Shack, Twister said to
Sam, "I guess I made a Squid-eo after all.
You are the star.
Otto and Reggie are your co-stars."

"Climbing is not about who is best,"
Sam said. "It's about you and the rock and—"
"I know, I know," said Twister.

"Hey, Squid, how did you get this good?"

Otto asked.

Sam looked at Tito. Tito winked at him.

"Practice, practice, practice," said Sam,

winking back.